I SPY LIFE ON THE FARM

I Spy Life on the Farm

ISBN: 9798711033851

Printed in the USA

I SPY with my little eyes,
something beginning with...

A is for
Apple

I SPY with my little eyes, something beginning with...

B is for

Barn

I SPY with my little eyes, something beginning with...

C is for
Chicken
D is for
Duck

I SPY with my little eyes, something beginning with...

E is for

Egg

I SPY with my little eyes, something beginning with...

F is for
Farmer

I SPY with my little eyes, something beginning with...

G is for
Goat
H is for
Horse

I SPY with my little eyes, something beginning with...

I is for

Irrigation

I SPY with my little eyes, something beginning with...

J is for

Jam

I SPY with my little eyes, something beginning with...

K is for
Kitten

L is for
Lettuce

I SPY with my little eyes,
something beginning with...

M is for
Milk

I SPY with my little eyes, something beginning with...

N is for
Nest

I SPY with my little eyes,
something beginning with...

O is for Orange

P is for Pig

I SPY with my little eyes, something beginning with...

Q is for
Quail

I SPY with my little eyes, something beginning with...

R is for
Rooster

I SPY with my little eyes, something beginning with...

S is for
Scarecrow
T is for
Tractor

I SPY with my little eyes, something beginning with...

U is for
Udder

I SPY with my little eyes,
something beginning with...

Vegetables

I SPY with my little eyes, something beginning with...

W and X

W is for
Windmill
X is for
X-ray

I SPY with my little eyes, something beginning with...

Y is for
Yam

I SPY with my little eyes, something beginning with...

Zucchini